THE HOLY LAND

Pär Lagerkvist

THE HOLY LAND

Translated from the Swedish by Naomi Walford

Illustrated by Emil Antonucci

Vintage Books

A Division of Random House New York

First Vintage Books Edition, March 1982

Library of Congress Cataloging in Publication Data
Lagerkvist, Pär, 1891-1974.
The Holy Land.
Translation of: Det Heliga landet.
Originally published: New York: Random House, 1966.
I. Title.
PT9875.L2H3813 1982 839.7'372 81-16147
ISBN 0-394-70819-9 AACR2
Manufactured in the United States of America

THE HOLY LAND

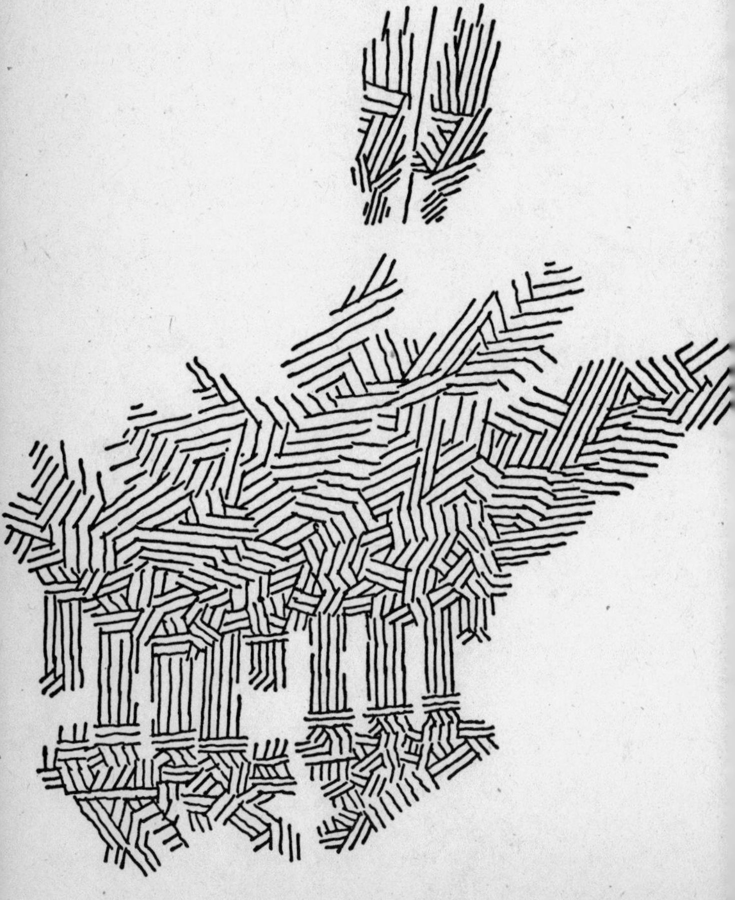

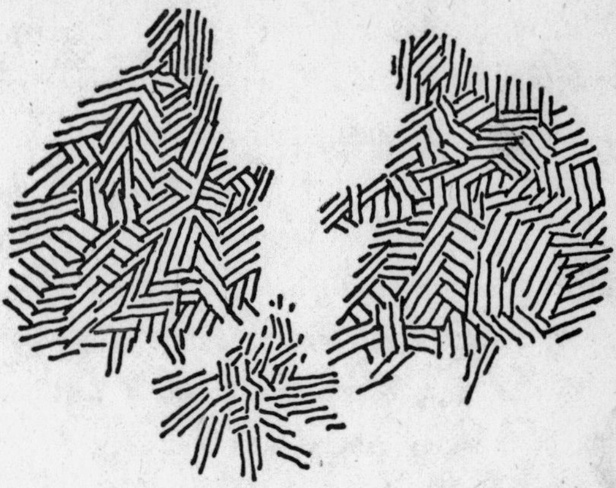

When Giovanni grew old and blind he was set ashore on a desolate coast, for he could be of no further use aboard ship, and Tobias went with him. Dusk was already falling, and Tobias, who alone could see, looked about him for some human dwelling where they might spend the night. But no such thing appeared. All that could be discerned in that barren landscape were the ruins of some mighty pillars which, ancient and half-eroded, stood out against the tempestuous sky. These could offer but little shelter from the night chill and the fresh wind, but since there was no other place to make for, they set off towards them. With the blind man's hand in his, Tobias the pilgrim approached the ruined building, which rose, ravaged and abandoned, on that limitless shore where nothing grew but thistles and tall, parched grass. The blind man asked what sort of place it was that he was being taken to, but Tobias couldn't tell him, never having beheld such a building before.

By the time they came up to it darkness had fallen, and they groped their way forward between the columns and over fallen blocks of stone that barred their way and hindered them from entering. In the lee of what seemed to be the remains of a wall they at last found a place where they could lie down; and utterly exhausted they at once fell asleep.

Early in the morning when they awoke, Tobias looked about him in wonder at what had been their night's lodging.

"This can be no human dwelling," he said, and he tried to describe what he saw to his blind companion.

Giovanni stood up and passed his old hands over the mighty columns that soared to the sky.

"No, it can't be," he asserted. "It must be a temple. But a temple to a god that no longer exists. The stone is weathered away."

He stood looking about as if he were not blind at all, but able to perceive all the desolation that surrounded them.

"Suppose we've been so long at sea that all the temples are now abandoned and in ruins? And all the gods dead?"

"Would you really wish for such a thing?" exclaimed Tobias. His voice betrayed his agitation.

"Yes, indeed."

Tobias avoided his eyes, which, empty and expressionless, were turned towards him.

"Perhaps your wish has come true," he said.

He looked out between the riven columns and over the landscape, which was terrible in its utter desolation.

"I'll go and look for some fuel, so that we can light a fire," he said. "It's cold here in the dawn."

The temple seemed to have been surrounded at one time by a grove of trees, perhaps such as were sacred to the god, for here and there traces of them could be seen—chiefly roots that twisted along the ground and just beneath it, writhing like snakes among the tall, dried thistles that grew everywhere. Apparently the grove had been burnt down, for the roots were blackened as though by fire. Tobias broke up some of them without difficulty; it was harder to find such that were not too rotten. When he tore them loose the inside of them showed the same blackish-brown colour as the soil they had grown in. He also pulled up a little of the dry grass for kindling. Then he returned to the temple and the blind man.

The wind was still blowing, but in the shelter of the wall he at last succeeded in getting the fire to burn. It smoked a good deal because the fuel was so rotten and old—indeed ancient; one could hardly touch it without its crumbling to dust. Nor did it give much heat. Still, it was a fire, and Tobias tended it carefully, lest it should go out.

To judge by the remains of the walls, the place where they were sitting had once been a room; not a very large one in proportion to the great size of the building. Perhaps a sanctuary within the double rows of columns of which so little remained. Almost all the wall lay levelled with the ground, but one corner was still partly standing; it was here they had found shelter for the night and he had now lit their fire. They sat there, trying to warm themselves.

After a while they were greatly surprised to hear the sound of approaching footsteps and low voices, seemingly of two men. Soon afterwards the men came in through the fallen blocks of stone and up between the columns, where they halted without speaking. They wore faded brown cloaks and carried staves like herdsmen. That they were indeed herdsmen became apparent when a goat followed them in and halted to gaze at the strangers and their fire with the same wonder as theirs in its yellow eyes. The men hesitantly approached Tobias and the blind man and sat down by the fire. They had seen the smoke, they said, and marvelled at it. Marvelled that people should be living here—that this place with the ancient pillars should be inhabited.

They talked quietly, and their thin faces were kindly, as was their somewhat melancholy gaze. The goat began nibbling the dry grass in the room which might once have been holy. Now and then it raised its head and fixed its old eyes on them.

Giovanni asked what strange sort of building this might be, and whether it was a temple.

The herdsmen looked at each other, and one then replied that they did not know. It might have been, but they knew nothing about it. The pillars had always stood in this place, but they had no idea how or why.

"What seemed to us strange was that suddenly this morning there seemed to be people living here—that someone had built a fire among the pillars as if to dwell here. That was why we came."

"Yes, it may seem strange," Giovanni answered, "but we could find no other place—no human dwelling.

"Do you know to what god this temple was dedicated?" he went on.

"What god?"

"What god?" repeated the other herdsman, astonished. "No, we know nothing about that."

All were silent for a time.

Then one of the herdsmen asked very cautiously and hesitantly how they had come here, and where from.

"If you care to tell us," added the other.

Giovanni replied that they had come from the sea.

The goatherds seemed much surprised by this answer, which surely ought not to have been so unexpected. And Tobias, who alone was able to observe their surprise, could not account for it.

"Has no one ever come here from the sea before?" he asked.

"No, never."

"We were set ashore here from a ship," Giovanni explained after a while.

"A ship?"

"Yes. You must have seen ships at sea sometimes, even if they didn't put in here."

"No, never."

"That's extraordinary."

"Very extraordinary," echoed Tobias to himself.

"Why did you want to land here?"

"We didn't. We were set ashore against our will."

"Oh, I see."

The herdsmen exchanged glances of comprehension.

"So you didn't want to come here . . . We understand."

"You were out at sea, on your way to some other place—to something else—and were put ashore here instead."

"Yes, without food—without anything to live on," said Tobias indignantly. "Only a bit of bread," he added, drawing a piece from his pocket. "And this, which I stole, so that we could light a fire."

The herdsmen eagerly brought out large pieces of goat-cheese from leather pouches at their belts, and offered them to the two strangers. Tobias and the blind man began to eat; it was plain that they had had no food for a long time, and the fresh, sweetish cheese tasted good to them. They held it in one hand and the bread in the other, and were so engrossed in appeasing their hunger that they forgot to thank the men for what they had given them.

The herdsmen watched them with interest, and then, bending their heads together, began a whispered conversation.

Noticing this, Tobias asked them what they were talking about.

At first they made no reply; then they begged to look at what the two were eating—not the cheese, the other thing.

When they'd been given the bread they examined it closely, and then handed it back.

"Have you never seen any of this before?"

"No. We don't have it."

"Then what do you live on?"

"Oh, we have milk and cheese, and meat of course, from the goats and sheep. But nothing like that stuff you're eating."

Tobias asked them to taste the bread, but they wouldn't; they didn't want to take anything from them.

When the meal was over they began talking of other things.

"They must have been wicked people to treat you so."

"Well, yes," said Giovanni, "may be."

But Tobias replied in bitter resentment that they were indeed wicked: that they were wretches, criminals; that the ship had been a vessel of iniquity and the crew a gang of . . .

Giovanni tried to calm him, saying that they were like most other people, and shrugged his shoulders at Tobias's savage condemnation.

"And anyway we were part of them; we were members of the crew."

"What? You belonged to them?"

"Yes, we did. We can't deny it. Can we?" he demanded, turning to Tobias. "It's true, isn't it?"

"Yes," answered Tobias in a low voice.

They were silent for a time.

"But where were you bound for," asked one of the herdsmen, "in a vessel like that, with such people aboard?"

At first neither man answered. Tobias stared at the ground, and the blind man, whose gaze was really fixed on the herdsmen, just glared straight ahead with his empty eyes.

"To the Holy Land," answered Tobias suddenly, in a low, expressionless voice, as if unwilling to name it.

"The Holy Land?"

"The Holy Land? What land is that?"

But to this they received no reply. The herdsmen asked the question again and again, eager to learn of this country which they had never heard of, but Tobias made no answer and never looked up, while the blind man merely sat with his empty eyes upon them.

"The Holy Land," whispered the herdsmen to each other, and then they too fell silent. It was clear that they would have liked to know something about this country with the strange, unknown name, but they were to be disappointed. Perhaps the two strangers knew nothing about it either; they had never been there—never reached it.

Perhaps it was a country where no one had ever been.

Again they all sat for a while without speaking. The herdsmen, with their quiet, patient demeanour, seemed accustomed to sitting together in silence. They were worn old men, yet in some way they seemed ageless; one didn't think of how old they might be.

Then one of them, turning to Giovanni, said, "Aren't you blind?"

Giovanni nodded.

"How did it happen?" the other asked.

"We don't know," Tobias answered on the blind man's behalf. "Someone may have taken revenge upon him."

"Oh? Who?"

"Well—perhaps god."

"God?"

"Yes. But we don't know anything about that for certain."

"Why should the one you mentioned have taken such vengeance?"

"Because he'd blasphemed against him. But as I said, we know nothing about that for certain. I may just have imagined it."

One of the herdsmen turned to the blind man.

"What do you think about it yourself?"

"I doubt whether the one he talks of exists. But if he does, then I can well believe it of him."

Tobias seemed troubled by this answer, regarding

it perhaps as a further blasphemy; and the herdsmen too seemed not altogether pleased by the blind man's way of talking. They contemplated his powerful but aged face and big, heavy body. His broad chest was hairy, and among the grey hairs hung something on a worn chain: they wondered what it was.

"What's that he wears on his breast?" they whispered to Tobias, as if the blind man couldn't hear, though of course he heard that as clearly as anything else they said.

"It's a locket," replied Tobias.

This they evidently did not understand.

"A locket? What's a locket?"

"Well, nothing very remarkable in itself, perhaps. But it can hold something very precious—something the wearer cannot bear to lose. Therefore one wears it at one's breast, close to the heart, and can't endure to be parted from it."

"Oh."

"What does it hold, then?"

Tobias delayed answering.

"We understand. It must be a secret."

"Yes."

Tobias was silent for a little. Then he said, "It's empty."

"Empty?"

"Yes."

"Empty . . ."

"So it's of no value?"

"It's his only possession, and I've often noticed that he's afraid of losing it. I don't believe he could live without it."

"Although it's empty?"

"Yes."

"How strange . . . How can it be so precious when it's empty—when it doesn't contain what it ought to contain?"

"We don't understand. Can't you explain it to us?"

"Not everything can be explained. It just is so."

The herdsmen were silent. Their grave, rather tired eyes looked at the thing hanging among the grey hairs of the old man's chest, but they asked no more questions.

"Yes, yes," one of them whispered softly. "That's true. There are many things that can't be explained, but just are so."

More footsteps and voices sounded outside the temple, and the clatter of hooves; other herdsmen must be coming with their animals, attracted by the smoke from the fire. Already the goats were beginning to make their way in between the fallen blocks of stone, poking their pointed heads round the columns and observing the two strangers with their narrow gaze. Clearly it was the strangers they looked at and not the two herdsmen whom they knew well; their curiosity was aroused by the newcomers, who differed from the men they were used to. Flocks of sheep too were gathering outside and beginning to nibble the dry grass without looking about them. They did not enter the temple as the goats did. The men now came in sight and hesitantly approached the four by the fire. They made a sign of greeting but said nothing, and then sat down cross-legged in a ring round them, their staves across their knees. They seemed to be of about the same age as the other two, though it was hard to be sure; they had the same indeterminate air about them, and all one could tell was that not one of them was young or middle-aged: that all must have lived a long time.

The newcomers were unwilling to show surprise at the two strangers or ask any questions; but after a time the first two herdsmen began telling them what they had learnt from Tobias and the blind man about their strange adventure. The rest listened attentively, and they too seemed astonished that the strangers should have arrived from the sea, as if nothing could come from there. But what amazed them most was to hear that they had been on their way to the Holy Land—to something called by that name.

"The Holy Land?" they repeated softly, and looked at each other in wonder. What country might that be? They would have liked to know—to hear something about it. But the two herdsmen said no more of it, and offered no explanation—nothing beyond its strange name. Perhaps they knew no more themselves; perhaps not even the strangers did, since they had never reached it, and were simply on the way. The Holy Land . . . ?

They all pondered what manner of country this might be.

"Holy? What's that?" asked one of them, looking at Tobias and the blind man with his gentle old eyes. But he was given no answer.

Later the two herdsmen told them of the locket on the blind man's breast: that it was empty, but that he was afraid of losing it; that is should have contained something most valuable, but did not;

and that it must be grievous to wear, since he knew it to be empty. He was surely not a happy man, although he carried so precious a thing at his breast; and someone unknown had wrought revenge on him, which was why he was blind.

Giovanni appeared quite indifferent to what they were saying, but whether he really was or not, no one could tell.

After that there was no more talk; the herdsmen remained sitting for a time in the silence that was so natural to them. On leaving they expressed kind offers to help the strangers with whatever they could get for them—though that was little enough, they added apologetically. Then they all went away. The goats, which had made themselves quite at home in the temple, rubbing themselves against the altar and the pillars, and nosing and sniffing everywhere, went too; they jumped agilely out between the blocks of stone and in among the sheep, which then moved away across the plain with the herdsmen in their midst. Giovanni and Tobias remained alone beside their fire.

They sat there until the last ember had died, and all that happened was that a completely bald man poked out his little birdlike head from behind one of the columns and observed them with swift, birdlike glances. Then he withdrew as unnoticeably as he had come. Tobias never saw him; only the empty eyes of the blind man had been turned upon him, unseeing.

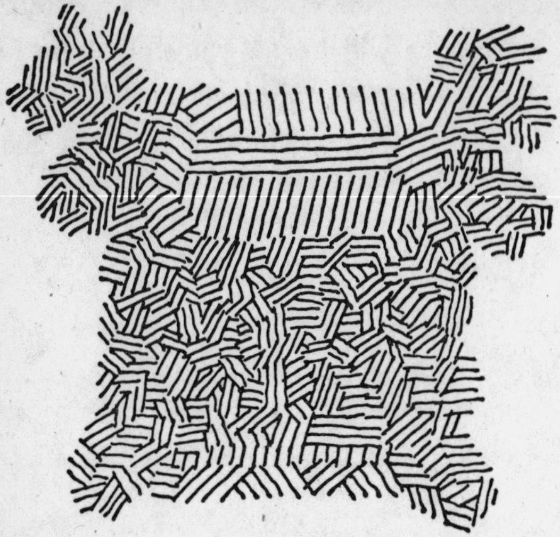

Tobias and Giovanni now dwelt among the herdsmen, and shared their life on that desolate, wind-tormented strip of sea-coast, except that they had no flocks to tend and lived in the ruins of the old temple instead of a hut made of reeds and yellow-brown clay such as the herdsmen had built for themselves, and which were barely distinguishable from the landscape. These neighbours often visited them, bringing cheese and goats'-milk and dried mutton or sometimes fresh meat, which Tobias cooked on his fire. Sometimes they brought herbs of various kinds, and taught him to make a very savoury soup which was said to be quite wholesome. Those plants grew only in certain places and were difficult to find, especially the one that gave the fine flavour. When Tobias asked what they were called, the men said they had no names for them; they just knew where they grew. Perhaps in times gone by they had had names, but if so they were now forgotten. On such visits the men would sit and chat—not for long, but long enough to show that for all their silent ways they liked to talk. They spoke of their life, of their daily work and of how they often had to drive their animals great distances to find pasture. The hardest thing was to find water, for nearly all water holes dried up in the constant wind.

Tobias once asked who owned the flocks that they tended. They replied that so far as they knew, no one did. Perhaps at some time they had belonged to someone, but that must have been very long ago.

So the flocks were now theirs?

No, they didn't think so. No, surely not.

They said goodbye in their quiet, friendly fashion, and went away, leaving the two alone in their temple.

This had now become their home, and the herdsmen grew accustomed to seeing the smoke rise up from it as from any other dwelling. According to what the strangers had said, it had not been intended for people but for someone else; though what they meant by that no one could understand.

Tobias and Giovanni settled down in this home of theirs, though it gave scanty shelter against the wind and the night cold. Tobias improved it a little by building a bank of turf to protect their hearth and sleeping-place on the side where there was no wall. He did other things too for their convenience and comfort, so that the dwelling-place in the corner of the former temple-cell became more and more like a human habitation.

He also made a closer examination of the temple, and described it to the blind man, who had better knowledge of ancient things though he now lacked eyes to see them with. Then he found, not far from what they called their home, a square structure of richly sculptured stone, its sides covered with secret symbols and carvings, and with strange, almost ferocious heads of animals at the four top corners. He led the blind man to it, and guided his old hand so that the trembling fingers might follow the carved signs and feel the animal-heads, which had horns curved like rams', and sneering, half-open mouths.

"This must be an altar," he said. "Here they must have made sacrifice to the god who lived in the temple—the god to whom it was dedicated. It seems better preserved than anything else in his house; why, I don't know. But in all temples the altar was the holiest thing."

They also discovered that the temple itself was built of volcanic rock, and so had borne within it the elements of its own destruction—its erosion and destruction. But the altar was of a hard, enduring kind of stone which Giovanni believed must be marble, although ravaged and—from what Tobias said—much darkened; almost brown from wind and weather.

"Some things live long," said the old blind man, "and others quickly vanish."

In this way they came to know the place—the holy place where they had taken up their dwelling. They grew accustomed to it; they grew accustomed to sitting and listening to the sough of the wind between the half-eroded columns and among the dry thistles between the fallen masonry. In the evenings Tobias often sat gazing over the desolate plain where, in the distance, herdsmen drove forth their flocks.

But seaward he never looked, though it was from

there that they had come. Nor was there anything to be seen in that direction—not a sail, not a vessel of any kind. Like the herdsmen, they ceased to think about the sea or to expect anything from it.

Yet Tobias did sometimes look towards the mountains that bordered the strip of coast on the landward side. They were strange, he thought, and somehow unreal. What secrets might they hide? They lay in a perpetual dusk or half-light, and one could make out nothing of them except that they seemed quite bare and that a narrow path appeared to wind alongside and over them; but this track was vague and hard to discern.

Tobias often stood looking up at the path which might or might not exist.

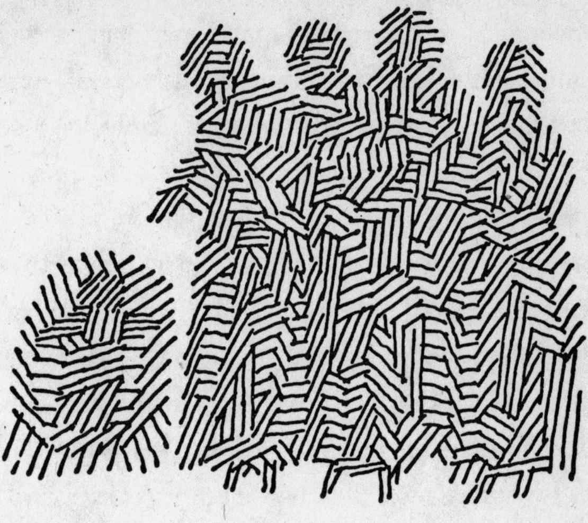

One day the herdsmen prepared a great surprise for the two strangers. More of them appeared than usual, and behaved rather oddly, whispering among themselves and finding it difficult to say just what it was they wanted. At last it became clear that they had something to show them—a secret that until then had been well kept. Not by a single word had one of them betrayed or even hinted at it. But now they had evidently overcome their doubts and agreed to initiate the strangers.

They all set off from the temple towards the mountains, in a direction that Tobias had never before taken. Almost at the foot of the hills was a brushwood cabin which would certainly have been difficult to find without a guide. As they approached, a man stepped out of the opening of the hut and made a wordless sign of greeting, as was the custom among these people. He was dressed as a herdsman like the rest of them, but being no more than middle-aged, differed from them very much. His face was serene and open; he smiled at them in a friendly, rather shy way and regarded the two strangers with grave, dark brown eyes. A few of the herdsmen talked quietly to him, and he nodded in assent. Then one of them went forward, cautiously drew aside the rush mat from the entrance and looked inside. He fell on his knees as if in reverence to something within, though it may only have been to see better. Other herdsmen also went up and looked in, and a couple of them knelt like the first.

Tobias could make nothing of it. But now one of the men led him to the doorway that he too might see. He bent down in the dimness and was able to discern something of the interior of the cabin.

There in a basket of woven willow, on a fine bed

of straw, lay a baby, waving its arms and kicking out with its bare, chubby legs, evidently pleased that so many people had come to see it. Its eyes shone eagerly at them, and it smiled happily, showing the beginnings of two white teeth in the upper jaw. It was plain to see that this was a boy, for he was quite naked, and he clenched his little fists very vigorously as he brandished them. He looked healthy and well-nourished, and in the corners of his mouth were traces of goat's-milk.

Sometimes he cooed contentedly, and once he grasped a finger that one of the old herdsmen held out to him. The man was overjoyed at this, and moved almost to tears.

When all had seen what the hut contained, they were evidently most curious to know what Tobias would do, what he thought of the child and how he would express his admiration of him. That he must admire him they had no doubt. And he did, speaking of him as enthusiastically as he could.

Yet perhaps he didn't quite come up to the old men's expectations, for he was so full of wonder at the scene that his thoughts were busier with that than with what he was saying. He soon fell silent, and they wondered why he said no more.

No one understood what was stirring in him—what memories were rising up before his mind's eye and filling him with thoughts that he would have found it hard to express. And no one would have understood if he had tried. He just gazed abstractedly before him. At the entrance to the hut two more herdsmen kneeled, drew aside the rush mat and looked in.

Beside Tobias stood the blind man. He was bewildered, not knowing what was going on around him, and unable to guess at it from what was said. Tobias whispered something to him; then, taking his hand, he led him forward to the entrance as if to let him look in. Again he whispered, and tried to explain what it was that filled them all with such joy, but to little avail. To the blind man the hut was full of darkness, and he understood nothing.

Now the herdsmen asked the father to tell the strangers how the baby had come down here to them, and about the mother, who was no more. For the mother was dead, they explained, so that the child now had only them. His father and them.

And the father began to relate, a little hesitantly at first, how the baby had been born up in the mountains, in a tract of country quite different from this. The mother had been happy while she was carrying him. Everything had been perfect at that time. She had felt calm and confident, and life seemed to her rich as never before, for she not only beheld it about her but bore it within. Yes, this was a child that really made his mother happy.

The birth had been difficult, and during the short time she survived she must have suffered much, though she never showed it. Nor did she betray how she suffered at the thought of having to die—if indeed she did. No one ever knew what she felt at being forced to leave life in the flower of her youth. But the strange thing was that when she felt the end approaching, she asked that the babe might be laid at her breast and lie there when she died, so that—as she said—it might learn to know death from its own mother. And this was done. But the father wondered greatly at it.

When the mother was dead, he heard an inner voice telling him to take the child on his arm and go down the mountain to live among the people there. But why he had heard this voice, and why he was to do this thing, he did not know.

The herdsmen were always much distressed by the last part of his story. They loved to hear the beginning, but not about the child at the dead mother's breast. And they began urging the father in the liveliest manner to take really good care of the baby, and never leave him alone. They would gladly take over his share of the herding so that he might stay with the boy, or at least remain close to the cabin. They also gave him advice and rules as to diet and so on, though they could hardly have known much about such matters. The father answered with his kindly smile that they need have no concern, and he refused their offer to help with the herding. He wanted to do his share like the others, and he never went very far from the hut. They listened but shook their heads, dissatisfied.

Then they went away, each to his own place.

When Tobias and Giovanni returned to their home in the temple, Tobias gave the blind man a minute account of what had happened in the cabin, and how the herdsmen had knelt before the child as if praying to it, though one couldn't say that they were really doing so. All the same—how strange! And how strange about that man who had come down from the mountains with the child on his arm so that it might live among them, and about the mother who seemed to have been the happiest, most radiant of women, yet who had initiated her child into death by laying it at her breast when she died.

Giovanni admitted that it was very strange, and for a long time he sat in silent reflection. Then he remarked that there were other divine children whose early life had been associated with herdsmen, besides the one that Tobias was evidently thinking of. But Tobias asked nothing about them; for him only one existed. And when evening came and they lay down to rest, he thought for a long time about the baby who now no doubt was sleeping safely and untroubled beside his father in the little cabin under the mysterious mountain. And he found that he too was anxious lest harm should come to it.

Until he fell asleep to the rustle of the wind in the dry thistles round the old ruined temple.

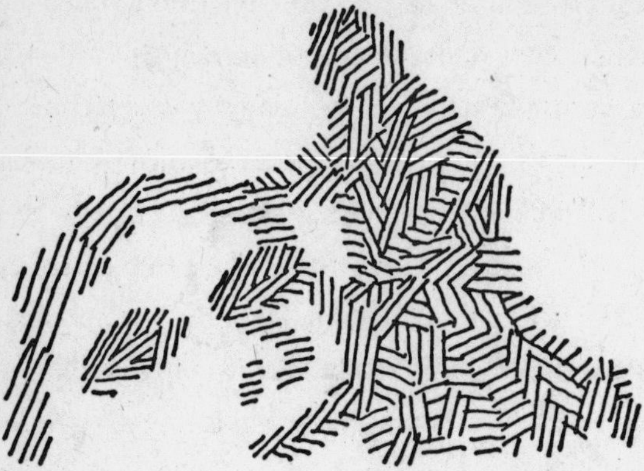

Tobias dug up a god.

A god which lay with its contemptuous smile to the ground. How long it had lain there, and what that smile really signified, no one could tell; neither Tobias himself, who was the first to see it, nor the herdsmen, nor Giovanni—who felt it with his trembling old fingers—nor the bald man who slunk in, having heard about the stone image, and who stood surveying it for a long time with his keen, bird's eyes, saying nothing. No one understood that ancient smile, or what secret it concealed; it was from too ancient a time. And indeed, had it ever been comprehensible to human beings? It was unconcerned, perfectly indifferent to the whole world of men, contemptuously averted from it—from everything. And yet—or perhaps just because of that—it made a frightening impression on the beholder, as did the whole of that massive stone face, its rough surface ingrained with brownish-red earth as with old blood. The stone from which it had been hewn was so dark that it seemed of a different kind from that of the altar, yet it may not have been. It lay within the remains of the old temple-walls, but in a place apart, where Tobias seldom went. It aroused his curiosity, for it was unlike the fallen stones, and appeared to have been worked in quite a different way from them. But what it represented he had no idea.

Nor had he now, when it stood upright again as perhaps it once did before being hurled to the ground by some power as unknown as itself. He didn't believe it was the image of a god; he couldn't think so. The only one who did think so was Giovanni: he who believed in no gods at all, or had no wish to. He said that god, if he existed, might well have that evil night aspect, and not just be the radiant and good and kindly being that people naturally preferred to believe. All that divinity, if there was such a thing, must be something far more comprehensive, more complex, than men could conceive of, and thus much truer. For the pure and simple was not—could not—be true. Only the complex could conceivably be that.

But had the temple really been dedicated to this deity? It was impossible to know. His image stood apart. The holy of holies, the altar in the cell itself, might have been designed for another. But god is not just one.

Now this stone face stood in its place again, watching them and all they did with indifferent, fixed eyes. At night it smiled its mocking smile off there in the darkness; the smile that had so long faced the ground because the image had been overthrown, but which was in no way changed on that account, and was still ingrained with red-brown temple earth as with old blood.

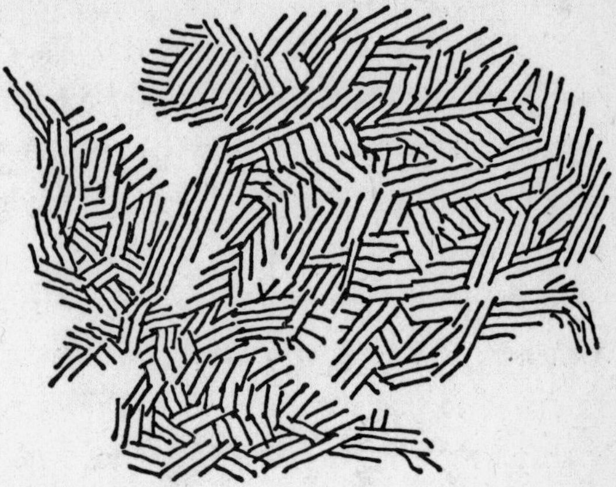

Great birds came flying in over the desolate coast-land, the land of the herdsmen; a few only at first, then more and more. Great, noiseless birds that glided on heavy, broad, motionless wings, with necks outstretched and heads turning almost imperceptibly to scan the land beneath. No one knew why they had come, or whence. It had never happened before; or if it had, it was so long ago that no one could remember it. They sailed overhead in ever increasing numbers, by day and night, and always noiselessly; it was almost frightening.

Then the reason for it appeared. They were found gathered about the carcasses of dead animals —sheep and goats—out in the pastures. A whole flock of them would feed off the same body, fighting over it, tearing at the flesh with powerful, hooked beaks, and watching each other with their yellow, venomous gaze. They never moved when approached, so that one could observe them and see exactly what they were like. They were quite different from what they seemed when gliding across the sky; they were a dirty yellow, repulsive, dusty-looking in their untidy plumage, which was plastered with nauseating scraps of carrion. Their heads were quite bald, and the granulated skin of their crops hung limp; they were hideous. These were no proud birds of prey as one might have thought, but obscene vultures.

They were impossible to chase off; they never stirred from the spot. And why should anyone chase them? The dead animals emitted such a stench that it was as well they should be devoured; the vultures left nothing but clean, white bones.

But why were the animals dying? This the herdsmen did not understand at all. Why had this disaster befallen them? They had tended their beasts exactly as usual—as they had always done for as long as they could remember. Why was this thing happening?

They were shocked by this change in their world, and troubled as never before.

More and more animals were found dead; they were easily detected because of the swarms of vultures that descended on them. The birds themselves were not easy to see, certainly, because they were of the same colour as the tussocky ground; but they moved and beat their yellowish wings as they ate and so revealed from a great distance that yet another animal had succumbed—had fallen victim to the disaster hurled at them from space, from heaven. For the herdsmen regarded this affliction not as a disease but as a blow of fate, incomprehensible because nothing like it had ever happened before.

The two strangers in the temple called it an epidemic; yet even to them there appeared something fateful and menacing about these inexplicable deaths, and these great birds that arrived in noiseless flocks as if from nowhere, seeming at first like proud envoys from a far and unknown country, only to reveal themselves as disgusting vulures led on their celestial flight by the stench of rotting carrion. And they too asked themselves: "Why is this happening? Why should anything happen in this land of uneventfulness?"

Who was that bald man? He appeared suddenly from time to time, and then he was gone again. For long periods they saw nothing of him at all. Where did he go?

Was he a herdsman? It hardly seemed so. It was difficult to imagine him tending a flock like the rest. He was not at all like them. Not in the least.

Sometimes Tobias thought of asking them about him, but he never did. And the strange thing was that if he had, he would have been given no answer, or they would have answered evasively, as if they didn't know. Perhaps this was true. They may really not have known.

Now he suddenly appeared again. Where from? No one could tell, no one had noticed. He was just there. He was busy with something outside the temple, and a number of herdsmen gathered round to watch. Why had they come? How did they know he was there and what he was doing?

Tobias went out to see what was going on, but Giovanni, who had been growing feebler of late, remained on his bed of rushes in the temple, waiting to hear about it when his companion should return.

At first Tobias saw nothing. The herdsmen were standing in a close circle, and seemed not to like his pushing through to look. The bald man was there on the ground, his long thin hands grasping one of the detested birds; not so large a bird as the others, the ones round the carcasses. It was a young one with a broken wing; he had been able to seize it as it dragged itself along the ground. It lay now with both wings outstretched and its downy breast uppermost, helpless in the power of its tormentor, who evidently enjoyed torturing it. It struggled with all its might, but curiously enough uttered no sound. Not even when he broke its wings to make it lie still did it cry out. Rather than do that, it resigned itself to agony.

While grasping it he had held a knife between his

teeth, and now that he could let go of the bird he took the knife in his hand and slit the bird down the middle. Then he tore it in two halves, separated them and examined the entrails closely, while the little heart continued to beat. Not even now did the bird make a sound, and soon of course it was dead. But the bald man went on eagerly scanning the entrails, bending over them and looking like a bird himself, with his narrow, naked head and thin, stringy neck. Tobias thought the viscera looked clean and innocent, and oddly enough they gave forth no bad smell—no smell at all—although the wretched fledgling was of a breed that lived on carrion.

He found it hard to grasp the meaning of what he saw, but one of the herdsmen gave him some sort of whispered explanation. The bald man, who had knowledge possessed by no one else, was trying to find out what evil destiny had come upon them through these alien, evil birds, and how—if possible—it might be averted. That was why they were all so engrossed in what he was doing. And when Tobias studied the faces of the others he saw that they were excited, and that they were following the bald man's actions very tensely. But the queerest thing was that they seemed to experience a certain pleasure in watching the torturing of that wretched captive bird, and thus taking revenge upon it for what had befallen them. They were certainly unconscious of this, but their faces betrayed it. It was curious, for until now they had worn a gentle, peaceable expression, and Tobias had always associated this serenity with them. Now they looked altogether different, and it was impossible not to notice it.

When he went back to the blind man he told him what he had seen. To Giovanni, the bald man's behaviour seemed altogether deranged and without any connection with the past, though he may have fancied it had, perhaps in the belief that by means of his secret arts he would be able to reveal something of the mystery. But what interested Giovanni most was Tobias's account of the herdsmen, of the way in which their faces altered as they watched the young bird being tortured, and their gratification at being revenged upon something, however innocent. This tallied with his notion of mankind: a notion which these innocent men had sought to change by their gentleness and kindness, and by their adoration of the child that had come to them and lay in a cabin on a bed of straw, waiting to ring in his millennium.

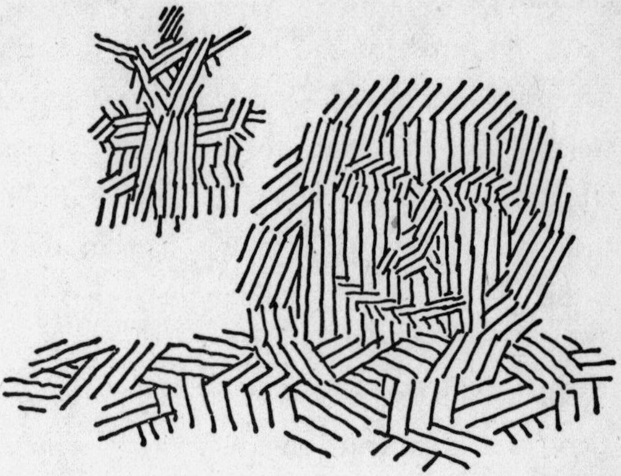

What the bald man had discovered by his rummaging in the entrails of the bird he of course did not reveal, but it must have had a bearing on the fact that some time later a lamb was sacrificed on the altar in the old ruined temple. There was no change in the sickness that raged through the stock, and something had to be done to avert the misfortune and propitiate someone—though who that someone was no one knew; certainly not the bald man who, standing at the altar, let the sacrificial lamb bleed to death as slowly as possible, so as to satisfy both the unknown and himself.

All the herdsmen had assembled in the temple; not just a few, but all. Quietly and reverently they watched this thing that they did not understand, while outside, almost as far as the eye could see, their flocks stood as if taking part in the rites within. No one had driven them there; they had just followed their shepherds.

The lamb allowed itself to be offered up without a cry, as if it understood what it was all about, and that this thing must be done. It did not resist like the young bird, which had struggled in its murderer's hands to the last. And once again the old altar was soiled with blood, innocent blood. Once again. And doubtless not for the last time.

Away in its seclusion stood the fallen and re-erected god, smiling its mocking smile at the scene.

And the sacrifice was in vain.

A woman walked down from the mountains. She carried a round basket woven of willow and containing a small poisonous snake. The basket was covered with a round lid, and she carried it in a sling that was also of willow. She walked slowly down the slopes in the blue-grey haze, and no one knew of her approach.

When she reached the plain the temple was straight ahead of her, though at some distance, and she continued towards it. Tobias was much astonished to see a woman approaching, and his astonishment was lessened when she stepped in to them between the pillars and in the most natural way sat down by their fire as if she had been expected. She gazed into the flames that licked up the temple wall, or what was left of it.

"This is no sacrificial fire," she said. "But that wood is of a kind that once was sacred. I can see that these are the roots of his tree, and that they burn unwillingly."

Her voice was deep, yet it was a woman's voice, and no man's.

"Why do you live here? This is not a house designed for people. And he left it long ago."

"We came here from the sea," said Tobias, "and not of our own free will. We were on our way to quite another country."

She nodded as if she had known this.

"Are you the pilgrim?"

"Yes," he answered, "or I was once."

Again she moved her head; it was as if she knew everything.

"And that blind man, who is he? He was surely not on his way to the Holy Land; that could hardly be."

"No," Giovanni himself answered. And although his voice was weak he spoke very emphatically, almost heatedly.

His strength was now so greatly diminished that he seemed unlikely to live much longer, but when an answer to such a question was required, all his old vehemence broke through.

"I was not on my way to anything at all," he added.

"I know. Yet you were set ashore here, and came to live in a temple, although it collapsed a long time ago. You seem pursued by your destiny."

"Destiny? I lie here on a bed of rushes somewhere in the dark, and whether or not it is a temple is nothing to me. For me there are no temples."

"Nor for me. I have seen too many fall, and I know that all them will fall in time. And after that? How will it be after that?"

"That doesn't concern me."

"Nor me. We can talk together, you and I, and it's seldom I can say that of anyone I exchange thoughts with. We understand each other. You have seen through many things, as I too have been forced to do—often without joy. Men cherish so many hopes—and to what end? Would they really be any happier if those hopes were fulfilled? Do you believe that?"

"No, and I never have believed it."

"Never?"

Giovanni made no reply. He seemed a little surprised at her way of talking, and being unable to see her face, could form no idea of who she was.

"You haven't always been the man you are now?" she went on.

"No, I suppose not. I've lived a long time."

"Yes, you must have. You look a little tired, as if you needed to rest now."

"I'm not tired. But everything must come to an end some time, if that's what you mean. Who are you, and why have you come?"

"I've come to release you."

"Release me? From what?"

The woman with the little plaited basket sat silent for a while. Then she stretched out her hand and touched the locket hanging amid the grey hairs on the old man's chest.

"What's that you're wearing?" she asked. "A locket?"

Giovanni raised himself a little as if to look, or to watch what she was doing.

She opened it.

"Do you know that it's empty?"

"Yes."

"And yet you wear it at your breast. That's strange, surely. Why do you?"

"I can't answer that. I don't know."

"No?"

"No. If you could tell me, you would make many things clear."

"Perhaps I could. But why should I?"

She closed the locket again, with a little snap.

But instead of laying it back among the grey hairs she gently removed it, lifting the thin chain over his head, murmuring softly, "Of what use is it?"

Giovanni's head sank back, and he was dead.

She stroked his forehead.

"Sleep now and rest," she whispered.

And his face looked calm, as if he had found a kind of peace.

Tobias rose up in agitation and came over to them.

"What have you done! You've killed him!"

But when he saw the old man's face he quieted and stood silent. He realised that something had been brought to fulfilment—something that had to be.

The locket on its thin, worn chain lay in the woman's hand, which was queerly furrowed and colourless. She looked at it and then up at him as he stood beside her.

"What shall we do with it?" she said. "It must be handed on to someone. Isn't that so?"

Tobias made no answer.

"Will you wear it?"

Tobias still said nothing, but when she held it out he knelt down and let her hang it about his neck.

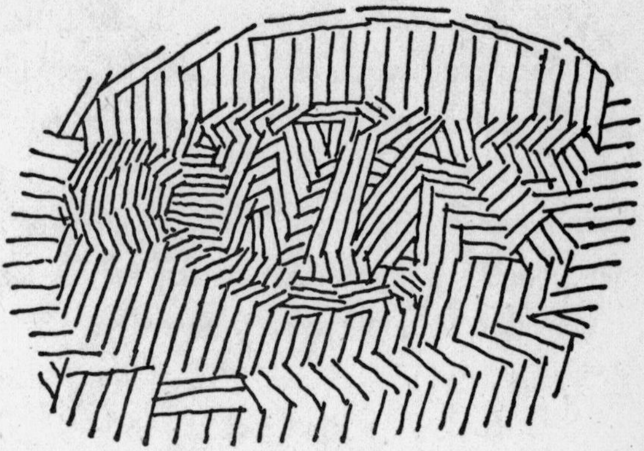

That same day, towards evening, the child in the cabin was found dead. It was the father who made the discovery when he came home, and he told the herdsmen. Strangely enough he did so very quietly, and without displaying any grief, they thought; he seemed almost to have been prepared for it—to have expected it—though this was not possible.

The herdsmen, on the other hand, were appalled. Their dismay and grief were so intense that they could scarcely contain themselves, though their self-control was the most noticeable thing about them. The event was entirely beyond their comprehension and the worst possible disaster. Such was their feeling. They had never been quite clear as to why the child meant so much to them, nor even now, despairing and full of grief as they were over their loss, did they reflect upon the strangeness of their devotion. They merely felt it. They felt an infinite emptiness now that the baby no longer existed in their world.

They rebuked the father for not having kept proper watch over the child, or for having failed to tend it as he should; for now the calamity that they had always feared and foretold had come to pass. But of what use were these reproaches? Moreover, they knew nothing of how the father had been negligent, if at all, being ignorant of the cause of death. The child had not been ill, and nothing about the little body gave any clue to what had happened—no suggestion of violence—nothing but a tiny mark on the left breast, too small to have any possible significance. The baby's death was unaccountable.

What they might have reproached the father for was that he seemed not to mourn as one might have expected: that he resigned himself submissively and quietly to what had happened. But this was something so extraordinary that they did not care to touch upon it. It was some sort of mystery. His attitude towards the child and to its death was quite different from theirs. He was not an outsider as they were; he was in some way initiated.

Tobias too came to look at the dead child, and like the rest he could discover no reason for its death. But when they showed him the little mark just under the left nipple he was so amazed and bewildered that he could barely hide his feelings—and the need to conceal them increased his confusion. For he perceived what none of the others had seen, far less understood—that that insignificant, innocent mark was a tiny snake-bite.

And he not only saw this, but understood what he saw.

When he and the woman from the hills had sat alone by the fire in the temple, she gazed into the flames for a long time without uttering a word.

Then, quite unexpectedly, she said something that astonished him.

"What child is it that the herdsmen worship?"

She spoke without looking up or turning to him.

On reflection it seemed to him not really strange that she should have known of this. And although her question was hardly a question at all, he replied that it was a baby in a little hut at the foot of the mountains. A man had come down from those heights carrying it on his arm, because the mother was dead and he had heard a voice telling him to do this. The mother was said to have been the most radiant of women, and yet when she was dying she asked to have the baby laid at her breast so that it might learn to know death from its own mother.

He answered thus without reflection. And indeed she knew it already, as well as he, just as she knew everything else. She nodded in assent, and asked no more.

But his curiosity as to who she might be increased still further after this. To his direct question she made no reply, and pretended not to have heard it. And when he asked whether she came from the mountains she merely nodded. More than that he never learned. They sat silently together by the fire and she stared into it the whole time. It was as if the flames captivated her because they sprang from the roots of trees that had once been sacred. Beside them, on the bed of rushes, lay the dead man—the once blind man—sleeping the very beginning of the endless sleep.

She had set down her basket on the trodden ground. From time to time there came from it a slight rustling, and Tobias wondered what could be causing it. But he knew that it would have been useless to ask her. Instead, hoping to discover at least some part of her secret, he cautiously raised the round lid, while she went on gazing abstractedly into the fire, and found that the basket contained a little snake, quite a tiny snake which looked at him with piercing eyes, its forked tongue protruding from its mouth. The woman noticed nothing, or did not care, and he replaced the lid too quietly for her to hear.

"It's very venomous," she said to his surprise, without turning. "But it has nothing to do with your destiny. That is too trivial, like all human destinies."

They sat for some time longer, and then she got up to go. Slinging her little willow-basket over her arm, she left him and the dead man.

"Are you going back to the mountains?" he asked as she walked out between the columns.

"Yes."

He heard her steps among the dry thistles outside the temple, and watched her moving further and further away across the desolate plain towards the hills.

Was he to blame for the child's death—or partly guilty of it? She would have found the little cabin anyway; she knew where it was. She knew everything.

But was he to blame? Partly to blame?

And what manner of child was it?

Not for anything so trivial as human destinies, she had said.

Who was she who deprived men of their hope—their only hope—by means of a little poisonous snake?

And did it joylessly.

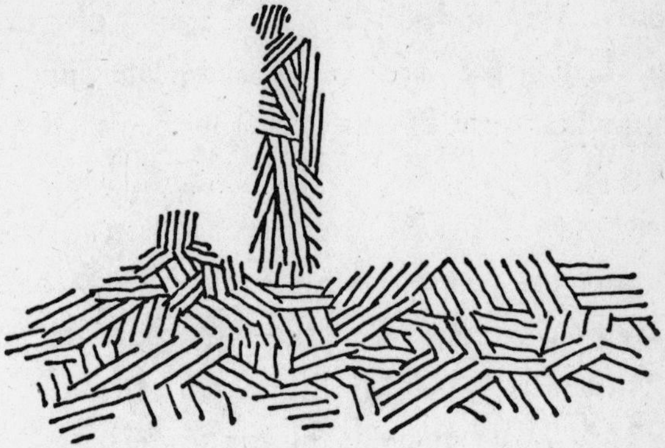

Giovanni's grave was dug outside the temple, beside what once must have been its entrance. At one moment Tobias wondered whether to place a cross upon it, but realised at once how mistaken, how wrong that would be. And no one here would have seen the point of such a cross—this symbol for something they knew nothing about, and which would have been very difficult to explain to them.

Tobias often sat beside the grave, plunged in reflection. He thought of the man resting down there, and of how appropriate it was that he should lie in this ground that had once been holy but was so no longer. He who had blasphemed against everything in which he had once believed, and while sailing the boundless ocean had so stubbornly denied that he was on the way to anywhere. Now he had at any rate attained to some sort of goal at last; he would become one with this soil that remembered nothing and would enclose him in the embrace of the great oblivion: surely mankind's final home. Or was it?

Thus he sat thinking by the grave outside the ruined temple, with the empty locket about his neck. The locket that must be worn by someone; the locket that had passed to him from the old blind man who rested there.

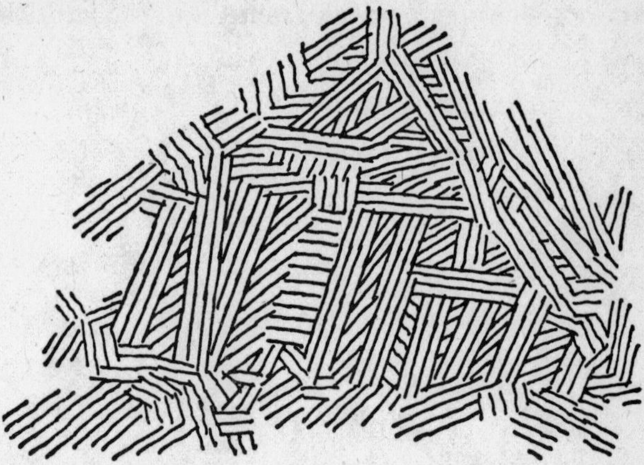

The sickness among the livestock ceased after a time, and the great bald-headed birds departed as silently as they had come. The life of the herdsmen on that desolate coast with its continual, tormenting wind continued as before, except that the cabin at the mountain's foot was empty. The father was no longer there. No one knew when he had left it, or where he had gone. Perhaps he had lifted the dead child in his arms and walked away as quietly and unseen as he had come. But they knew nothing.

The cabin was soon blown down, for it was built of brushwood and no one tended it any more; soon no trace of it remained.

He who has once been a pilgrim must always be ready to move on, to set forth on his journeying again. It is of no use to say: "No longer. I'm no longer a pilgrim."

You were one once. Weren't you?

Now the path of the pilgrim awaits you again. Move on! Move on!

Tobias stood there by his temple—not his at all—looking up at the hills, the mysterious hills with their blue haze; the hills that the child was said to have come from, and from which the snake-woman had descended to deprive the herdsmen of their hope, and the blind man of his one possession.

The snake-woman . . . Strange—he could not recall her face. He remembered her vividly; no one he had ever met had left so deep an impression on his memory. But her face he could not remember. It was as if he had never seen it—as if she had had no face. And of course she had stared away from him and into the fire throughout.

"What child is it that the herdsmen worship?"

And he had told her . . .

Guilty? Partly guilty? Was he guilty also of this? What accusations were these that assailed him . . . And memories . . . memories from the distant past . . . blood-memories! . . .

Move on! Move on!

The child . . . The child who learned of death from its own mother . . . What terrible memories were these that were revived in him . . .

Move on! Move on! Pilgrim, move on to atone for your crime, to win expiation, to win peace in your soul . . .

Miscreant, move on!

It was morning when he began his journey up the mountain, yet everything there lay in blurred haze—a blue-grey haze—so that it seemed evening. Was it always evening here? He didn't know; he knew nothing of this mountain and its mysterious heights, which were as mysterious and veiled now that he was up among them as when he had beheld them from a distance. Should he climb up into this mist to gain clarity? To win certainty about himself and his destiny? The destiny of mankind?

He walked along something that was a perhaps a path, perhaps not. Everything here was unreal—even a path that one walked along, that one pursued uphill in quietness, in the perfect stillness and silence that prevailed here. No wind—not the faintest breath—and this felt strange to one coming from the land of the herdsmen. Did no wind blow up here? Was there no murmur in grass or tree? No, here was neither tree nor blade of grass. And no wind to sough through them. Nothing. Here was nothing.

Nor did time seem to be; for nothing changed. There came neither day nor night; it seemed always to be evening, half-dusk, a veiled twilight, a constant, changeless land of evening.

Because of the changelessness he had no idea how long he had been walking. He never lay down to rest, or felt the need of it. So far as he could tell, it cost him no effort to walk up the mountain. He did not weary. Then why did his heart beat so hard?

Why did he continually hear its thudding beat? He pressed his hand against it—against his chest—against the locket hanging there on its chain. Was that what made his heart so restless? An empty locket on a worn chain?

Of what use is it . . .

Yet when it was taken from him he could live no longer . . .

Upwards, upwards he climbed; up into the emptiness of the mountain and the land of evening. At last the path could be seen no longer; it could not be there. Perhaps it never had been there. Yet he went on excitedly—more and more excitedly. What was it that agitated him so? Something must be awaiting him, and he went on and on towards it, with a thumping heart.

Then, on a rise directly before him and above him, he beheld three empty crosses outlined against an ashen sky; a sky that he had never seen or thought of before, or knew existed. But now the hill and its three empty crosses were outlined against it. And it was as grey as ashes, with grey, tattered clouds, tumultuous, torn, yet entirely rigid, motionless, dead. A dead sky, a sky full of racing turbulence, but dead. Against it stood the three crosses. And they were empty.

He stopped and looked up at them with hot eyes, his mouth half open.

Then he went on again; he approached them, but more slowly. Halted again, stood still, and looked up.

Why were there three? Why not one?

Whose the middle one was one knew. Everyone knew that. But the two others, what business had they there? What had they to do with that past event? Criminals, two common criminals. Two murderers. Two common, human murderers. Why did he hang there with them? Why not with two decent people, innocent like himself? Or alone. Quite alone. But no. He was with two bandits who were entirely unknown to him. Why? Why should it be so?

He went yet nearer. Halted. Looked at the crosses, though not at the middle one.

Criminals. He was one himself. Murderers. He was one himself. Pilgrim and criminal. Pilgrim aboard the pirate ship of humanity, bound for the Holy Land. With all imaginable scum and riff-raff, himself being one of them. So it was. Such had been his life from beginning to end.

Three crosses. Not one.

Three crosses outlined against the desolate sky, changelessly, for all time—against a sky as dead as ashes. So it was. And so it would always be, as long as mankind endured.

Three crosses.

He went up to them.

Stopped before the middle one.

"This one is his. The innocent man's. That is not for me. I dare not touch it with my blood-soiled hand—not that one.

"But this," he said, and stepping to one of the others, he took hold of it. "This is the criminal's cross. The robber's cross. Mine. This I may touch, for it is not clean—no cleaner than myself, than my hand, and if there is blood upon it, it is the blood of a miscreant, like my own. I myself might have hung upon it."

He fell silent, and seemed deep in thought.

And yet—and yet. There the three crosses stood, all together; there was no denying it. Not just a solitary one—not just his. And not just the criminals' crosses. No; beside them was one that was said to be that of the son of god, and at any rate was an innocent man's. The criminals' crosses weren't solitary either. They stood there with his.

And so long as anyone—one single person—should remember this hillock, it would be remembered with three crosses on it. Never with one. Never with just his solitary cross. Always with those of the two criminals. Always with the three crosses together.

He looked up at them for the last time, seeing them against the sky that was empty and dead and grey as ashes. Was it already dead? Was heaven dead? Perhaps so. And yet the three crosses still stood out against it, should anyone wish to recall what had once happened, and ponder its meaning.

Then he came down from the hill.

He went in another direction—opposite from the way he had come; why, he did not know. The landscape here was somewhat different, though he could not have said how, and he never thought about it; he just felt that it was so. It was the same land of evening that he had walked through before, but as if it were in shadow, as if turned away—but from what? Perhaps there was more peace, more repose on this side of the mountain, which was not so steep, anyhow. He walked slowly down its slopes.

As before, he was unaware of time, or of how long he had been walking. He moved forward deep in thought—in the melancholy of those thoughts.

When at last he raised his eyes he saw that he was

approaching a river, a broad, calm river that flowed dark and mysterious through the land below him.

How did he know that it was a river? How could he know? He just felt it to be so.

The opposite shore was not to be seen, and no one could guess what might be hidden there. The river itself was swathed in dimness, so how could anything be known of the land beyond it?

He drew near to it slowly, for he did not go straight down the slope, but as it was natural to go, as a path would have wound and twisted; but there was no path. When at last he reached the bottom he saw a man standing on the edge with his back turned, right by the gliding water, as if deeply contemplating it.

Tobias was surprised, for he had met no other person here, nor—as he now realized—had he expected to. Who was it, who was this unknown man who stood with his face to the river and the night?

He went forward and stood beside him. Like him he looked down into the water. He saw his face reflected in it, but it was older, aged, with grey hair; he scarcely recognized it. He saw his own face reflected there, and only his. He saw that he was alone, that there was no one else there. That the stranger was himself.

He looked out over the dark water, over the river whose further shore was hidden, unknown to any.

"Not yet," he whispered to himself. "Not yet . . .

When he resumed his journey he did not continue along the river but inland again, for the shore was impassable; cliffs ran steeply into the water, forcing him to take another way. Thus he was parted from the river which had mirrored his face and which knew that it would soon do so again. He moved further and further from it and entered a valley that would certainly have been beautiful if there had been greenery and trees and flowers on its bare ground; but there was none. All life was swept away as if by a grey hand. On his way through this valley he came to a spring; that was what happened to him during his walk.

The spring lay just where he passed, to his left; he could not have gone by without noticing it. And perhaps this was the intention, the purpose, the thing destined. There it was in the bare rock, without a blade of grass or the least vegetation round it, and it was perfectly, transparently clear. One could see the bottom and everything in it quite plainly. It was not very deep.

He knelt down to drink, and as he bent over the cold surface he pressed the empty locket against his breast lest it should fall into the water. The water was very chilly and had no taste at all. No tang of moss or earth, no taste of metal, of rock or of anything else—of nothing earthly. Nor, so far as he could tell, of anything not of the earth. It was just pure and cool and good for quenching thirst. And he who drank of it knew that he would never thirst again.

When he resumed his wayfaring he pondered what manner of spring that might be. And he remembered another from which he had drunk in his youth: a spring with blood in it, carrying the tang of blood to the tongue.

Was that the spring of life? And if so, what was this? Not of death: that he knew. That was not yet . . .

He did not know what this spring was, or what it meant to have drunk from it.

. . .

His way now led him upwards, and it seemed to him that the light was increasing somewhat. He was no longer walking in a land of dusk but in a bright dimness that was less oppressive. The valley was less cramped, and was opening out, widening, as he followed the slope of the mountain. The ground was changing too, and seemed not quite so dead; and after a while he found himself following a path—an ever better-defined path—edged now by a little grass, and bushes of some sort—but what?

He went on and came to a place where a path from below joined the one he was following, and where they met stood a small wooden figure of a woman, with a little roof over it as if to protect it from rain. Could it rain here? Was this an ordinary, earthly region? Surely not.

The figure was very clumsily carved by a hand more pious than skilled, and—as it seemed—long ago. The gown was blue, but the paint had flaked off and was faded by wind and weather—as much as was left of it. But on the face the colour was better preserved. And the face was infinitely gentle, with a smile that was perhaps a little stiff because the artist had been unable to do better and to make it as he would have wished.

He paused and regarded the little figure; and in so doing—in looking at this little wooden woman in her blue wooden gown, so kindly smiling—he felt a touch of peace in his troubled soul.

Whom did she remind him of? That blue gown—the smile, the pale, kindly smile . . . What was he remembering? No, he couldn't capture it . . .

How strange—he felt suddenly tired, tired in quite an ordinary way, as one is after a long walk in the mountains. He must lie down to rest for a while, here in the grass beside her. So he lay looking up at her, at her gentle face, her kindly and perhaps rather sad smile, as he fell asleep.

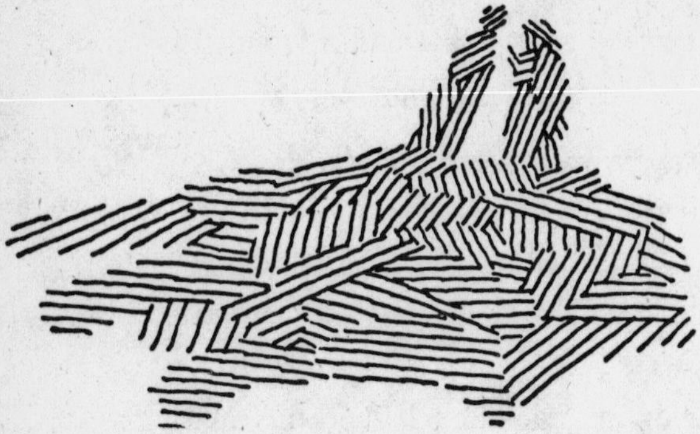

How strangely she was walking. Stiffly and unsteadily in a curious way, as if walking were difficult for her. Indeed there was something stiff and clumsy about her which he did not recognize. *She* had not walked like that. *Her* gait was light and natural, and she was so young—hardly more than a child—whereas the one beside him must be considerably older. But the dress was the same; the same pale blue colour, although hers had not been so stiff and wooden; she had made it herself and it became her very well; he would always remember her in it.

The voice was exactly the same: just as soft and low and not at all intrusive. One wasn't forced to listen to it, but one could if one liked, and hear how light and soft it was and how quietly she said everything.

But what she talked of was very strange, and not at all the sort of thing they used to speak of together. She said she was the mother of god's son—and that was odd; why did she talk about that and what had it to do with him? She had been chosen for that, she said, but not because there was anything especially remarkable about her. Some other woman might just as well have been chosen—one of the neighbours or a woman from another village. She bore him without knowing at all who he was, and when the shepherds came, and the three kings, she didn't understand. Nor had she any idea that he was to be crucified, and so she rejoiced over her child, like any ordinary mother.

But when it happened a sword went through her heart and since then she had never been the same. Since then she had indeed been chosen—but to suffer, and to understand others who suffered. So now she stood at every fork in the road, in case some passer-by wanted to stop and tell her of his sorrows and his cares.

"What is it that so saddens you?" she went on. "I noticed how downcast you were; I even stepped down to walk with you part of the way, and that I don't usually do."

"There is much to grieve over."

"You are right. Tell me what it is that so burdens you. And who you are and where you are going."

"I am a pilgrim."

"Are you?"

"Yes. Pilgrim and criminal."

"Criminal? What crime are you guilty of?"

"My whole life has been full of evil deeds. And evil thoughts, if one counts them too. I am the wicked man, the evil-doer, so you might as well call me that if you like. So there's nothing strange in my having to be a pilgrim."

"No, I understand that."

"But I'm an odd sort of pilgrim, you know. I'm on pilgrimage to a land that doesn't exist."

"How do you mean—doesn't exist?"

"To the Holy Land."

"The Holy Land . . . And that doesn't exist?"

"No. I realise that now."

"Doesn't exist . . . Are you sure of that?"

"Yes, I am."

"That's my own country—my homeland, you

see. But it's so long since I was there—so very long. And it doesn't exist? Are you telling me there's no such place?"

"Yes, I've found that out. I've found out that my pilgrimage has had no meaning, no goal."

"You grieve me very much by what you say. You see, I too have sometimes thought that there might be no such place. It feels so distant, so very far away . . . I've felt that more than once. And then I've thought perhaps it was just that I was standing here in a foreign country, at a road-fork in a foreign country, living in my memories and trying to comfort those who pass, by talking of them. But perhaps I'm talking about a land that doesn't exist at all; perhaps it isn't in the least as I remember it. And then I am heavy and sorrowful. Don't imagine that at times I am any less distressed and despairing than those I try to comfort."

"Now I've hurt you by what I said. Why should I do that!"

"You must say what you feel to be true, even though you should hurt me. But I'm familiar with all kinds of pain—even with the idea that my country may not exist. Even that.

"And yet surely it must? It's only now and then that it seems hidden from me; at other times I see it plainly. It's as if I were walking there along familiar roads that have now become holy. It may be my own fault that I don't always see it as I should; perhaps my eyes mist over now and then.

"You must have a home country too, and you'll know that one doesn't always recall it clearly."

"My home country? No, I hardly remember it at all. But no doubt that's because I don't want to remember it, for it would only revive evil memories."

"Evil memories? Only evil ones?"

"Yes. There's something there that I've always tried to forget, and for so long that now I can't recapture it . . . I can't get it clear in my mind. And yet I feel that I must be reminded of this thing before my wandering is over. You see, I haven't much time left, and I must be reconciled before the end. The river has reflected my face and I've drunk from the spring: I cannot have much time left . . ."

"No. I understand."

"I must meet her before my time runs out—before the light fades. Isn't it late? I mean, is dusk not falling?"

"Who is it that you're to meet?"

"The one you remind me of. The voice . . . and

the dress. But you walk so queerly; why is it so hard for you to walk? In a way you're not in the least like her. And you bore god's son. She never had a child. She ought to have, but never did—they forced her not to. This is what I don't remember—can't remember. Well yes, visiting that old woman—that dreadful old woman in that stale house, the grey house that smelt so stale. I went too—we held each other's hand—now I remember!—we were so frightened; we were no more than children ourselves, and we didn't understand—we didn't know anything of what we were being compelled to do. We just knew something about love, and thought we knew it all. Nothing of what was before us then, or even that such things existed, and that they too belonged to love.

"The smell of blood . . . I remember now . . . the smell of blood, and her screams. How she tried to defend herself. And the child—the baby that had to learn about death from its own mother . . . Now I remember! Now I remember! . . . that had to learn about death from its own mother!

"They forced her . . . so that there should be no life-fruit after me . . . nothing of their rich son in her womb . . . she who was so poor . . .

"Ah, now I remember it all! . . ."

"I know whom you mean. She has often talked to me; for she is one who really needs consolation.

"She has spoken of you many times, too."

"Of me? Then she must have used hard words, the hardest there are."

"No, she has never said anything but good of you."

"That's not possible."

"Oh yes, it is possible—for those who love."

"Love . . . ? What do you mean? That she loves me?"

"Yes. And she doesn't judge you. Love does not judge."

"It's impossible. I left her alone with her despair—they forced me to that too, but why did I obey them? I needn't have obeyed them! And they found her at the edge of the river in her blue linen dress, in her fine dress, her only one, made of flax that she had sown and harvested, and they carried her up to the village and buried her outside the churchyard wall; for she might not lie within it among the others, the righteous people. I watched them bury her—two men. I was crouching behind some bushes, and saw it. And when they had filled in the grave and gone away I slunk from my hiding-place and threw myself on the grave mound, and wept and wept . . . But she was no less lonely for that.

"Then my evil ways began, and continued for a long time afterwards—far too long. That's how I've been my whole life, my whole criminal life . . ."

"You speak too harshly of yourself. You've been a pilgrim too, you said. That too."

"Pilgrim . . . a pilgrim too . . . Oh yes . . . but how has that changed me? Have I become another person? Easy enough to be a pilgrim if one doesn't have to alter—if one can stay the same as one was before. A pilgrim—to a country that doesn't exist; that for safety's sake doesn't exist—that one can never reach.

"That one need only long for."

"Yes. Only long for. You're right. And that's not enough."

"No. But that's how it is for me. No more than that."

"Then I can't help you. I don't think I can help you . . ."

He walked deep in thought, his own thoughts and those that she had given him—that her last words had suggested. There was good reason to reflect upon them . . .

He was on the point of saying something about this—more about it—when he noticed that she was no longer beside him; someone else was walking there—in a blue dress, in the blue dress that she herself had made—had woven and sewn—of flax that she herself had harvested . . .

"I have been waiting for you," she said in a low voice. "Now you've come—at last."

"Yes. I'm an old man now. I looked at myself a little while ago in a dark river, and saw.

"How young you are. It's extraordinary. Is it because you're dead?"

"Young? I don't know anything about that. Young? Perhaps."

"It must be hard for you to meet me again."

"Yes. But it's what I've longed for all the time."

"And so have I. I've dreaded and longed for it all my life. I could win no peace until I met you again. But how can you give me peace? How can you wish it for me?"

"I wish that everyone may have peace—you above all, who have such need of it.

"Are you tired? You seem so."

"Yes. I have journeyed for a long time."

"Then I think you should lie down for a while. I will sit beside you while you rest."

"Yes. I would like to do that. And it's getting late. Isn't dusk falling?"

"I can't tell you. I know nothing about such things."

"No, I understand . . ."

"What's that on your breast? A locket . . ."

He made no answer, but raised his head a little.

"There's nothing in it. It looks as if there ought to be, but there's nothing."

"No, there's nothing . . ."

She closed it again. And gently, gently she took it from him, lifting the worn chain from his neck and putting it about her own; she hung the empty locket at her own breast. At that moment it began to shine like the most beautiful jewel.

But as he beheld this, his old head sank back upon the ground, and he was dead.

With infinite tenderness she stroked his forehead.

"Sleep now, and rest," she whispered.

And his face seemed full of a great peace.

Lagerkvist's purity of thought and mode makes his writings look deceptively simple; in truth they are the intense, forceful utterances of a mind which has explored many artistic trends before arriving at the singular form which identifies its work, or the complex philosophy pervading it.

Perhaps most significant in the Swedish author's progress was a trip made to Paris in 1913. At that time he came under the influence of the French art world, then flirting with cubism and expressionistic designs. Seeking to employ such virility and power in his own writing, he opposed the naturalistic bent of his predecessors and developed a leaner, more disciplined style. In the years following he has continued to experiment with methods of presenting his enormous, universal themes, in plays, short stories, novels, poems and essays. Whether or not one always agrees with his concepts, often moving toward the existential, one must admire his humanistic purposes and the lucid beauty of his prose.

In 1940 Lagerkvist was elected one of the eighteen "immortals" of the Swedish Academy, and a decade later received the Nobel Prize for Literature.